# Young Dracula

## by

## Michael Lawrence

## Illustrated by Chris Mould

You do not need to read this page - just get on with the book!

First published in Great Britain by Barrington Stoke Ltd
10 Belford Terrace, Edinburgh EH4 3DQ
Copyright © 2002 Michael Lawrence
Illustrations © Chris Mould
The moral right of the author has been asserted in
accordance with the Copyright, Designs and
Patents Act 1988
ISBN 1-84299-051-9
Printed by Polestar AUP Aberdeen Ltd

# MEET THE AUTHOR - MICHAEL LAWRENCE

*What is your favourite animal?*
The Griffin
*What is your favourite boy's name?*
Hieronymous
*What is your favourite girl's name?*
Erthrulda Bog
*What is your favourite food?*
Moussaka (with icy Greek beer)
*What is your favourite music?*
Tibetan mountain music
*What is your favourite hobby?*
Pogo-sticking in the Himalayas

# MEET THE ILLUSTRATOR - CHRIS MOULD

*What is your favourite animal?*
Lizard
*What is your favourite boy's name?*
Chris! It's so cool, like me.
*What is your favourite girl's name?*
Emily and Charlotte (my two daughters)
*What is your favourite food?*
Curry
*What is your favourite music?*
I love all kinds of music
*What is your favourite hobby?*
Drawing!

For Megan Larkin,
my greatest critic

# Contents

# Chapter 1
# Wilfred the Bold

I'm sure you've heard of Count Dracula, the evil vampire who could turn himself into a bat at will. The creepy fellow who always dressed in black and preferred a neckful of warm blood to a mug of milky tea any day.

Yes, everyone's heard of Count Dracula. But how many of us know what he was like when young? Before he grew tall, swept his

hair back, and started hanging round graveyards? Not many of us! And why? Because until now, the story of young Dracula has been a well-kept secret – a secret that I (a very nosy writer) have at last unearthed.

Before I tell you this secret story, however, you must learn something of life at Castle Dracula before the lad was born. Pay attention now. This bit's important.

In a remote corner of Transylvania, there were once two rival vampires. One was Count Dracula, the other Baron Gertler. The Count and the Baron lived in tall, black castles on opposite sides of the valley.

Far below, between the two castles, there was a village.

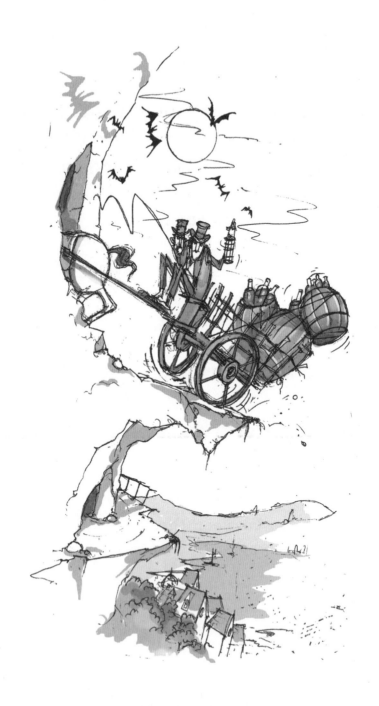

Every night, very late, village bloodmen
(the Transylvanian version of milkmen)
rode up to the castles with bottles of fresh
blood for the Count and the Baron. The
bloodmen collected a cupful from everyone
in the village between the ages of ten and
eighty. The villagers had no choice in this.

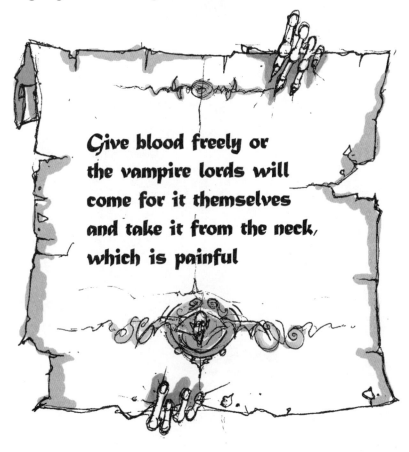

**Give blood freely or
the vampire lords will
come for it themselves
and take it from the neck,
which is painful**

Now, Count Dracula and Baron Gertler were the last of their line. Neither of them had children to follow in their bloody footsteps. But one year, the Count brought home a wife, and the following year Countess Dracula gave birth to a son, whom they called Wilfred.

When Baron Gertler heard that the Draculas had an heir, he became very jealous. He turned himself into a giant bat, flew to the castle across the valley, and snatched the babe from his mother's arms while the Count was clipping his toenails in the bath. Then he flew off with the child under his arm.

The distressed Countess rushed to the window to save her darling son, but reaching for him she leant out too far and tumbled to her death far below. Her scream brought the Count dripping from the bath.

As soon as he saw what had happened, the Count ground his vampire teeth with rage, turned himself into a bat, and flew after the Baron. The Baron escaped, but the Count managed to save baby Wilfred and bring him home.

Some nights later, the Count sneaked into Castle Gertler before the Baron was up, and hammered a wooden stake through his mean old heart.

Twelve years passed. Count Dracula was now half the vampire he had been. He was lame and could no longer turn himself into a bat. He never went out at night. The villagers no longer feared him, and the bloodmen no longer delivered. He had to content himself with the blood of the rats that scampered around the castle.

One dark and miserable midnight, the old Count sat gazing out from his high tower. On the hill across the valley stood the crumbling ruin of Castle Gertler. No-one had lived there since the Baron's death.

"Ah, those were the nights," the Count sighed, with a tear in his eye.

He missed having a real enemy. He missed being young and fit enough to go out for a neck or two of human blood when the fancy took him. There wasn't even anyone to talk to now. No-one that mattered anyway. It was no use talking to Wilfred. They had nothing in common, nothing at all.

"Are you all right, Father?"

The Count jumped. He hadn't heard Wilfred come up the stairs. "Oh, it's you," he snapped. "What do you want?"

Wilfred was worried about the old vampire. He was a kind and sensitive lad.

"I was wondering if you'd like a bowl of toad and tomato soup, Father."

The Count scowled. "No, Wilfred, I do not want soup. I want blood, gently warmed, bit of froth on top, no sugar. If you had any thought for your poor old father you'd go down to the valley, drag a villager out of bed, and drain his blood into a jug for me."

"But Father, I hate doing that, you know I do."

"To think," the Count said, "that one day you'll be head of the House of Dracula. Why, I wouldn't be surprised if the first thing you do when I'm turned to dust is put up pretty curtains and put flowers everywhere. You're not a vampire, Wilfred, you're a wimpire!"

Wilfred was badly stung by these harsh words. He so wanted to be like all the

Draculas before him. Was it *his* fault that he was different? He went down to his room and climbed into his coffin, where he tossed and turned sadly for a while.

At last he fell asleep. Wilfred had always had trouble keeping awake at night – another thing that upset his father. The Count was old-fashioned. He believed that vampires should sleep during the day and be up all night, sipping the red stuff.

The good thing about sleeping at night, from Wilfred's point of view, was the dreams. Night dreams were sweeter than day dreams. Tonight, for instance, he dreamt that he didn't have to live in a cold and gloomy castle or file his teeth at coffin-time.

In the dream, he didn't feel a wimp for preferring milk to blood either. He had a cow all of his own.

Lying beneath her in the straw and dung, he could drink fresh, warm milk to his heart's content.

In this wonderful dream, Wilfred ran through open fields in broad daylight, singing at the top of his voice. Sunlight didn't make him cry out in pain the moment it touched his skin, as it would in real life. In the dream, he was the Wilfred he longed to be.

But when he woke, the dream vanished and the gloom of the Castle settled about him once more. The Count's unkind remark came back to him: *"You're not a vampire, Wilfred, you're a wimpire."*

Wilfred sighed. "I so want Father to be proud of me," he said, and resolved to go out and prove that he was a true vampire after all.

He waited indoors all that day, hiding from the sunlight which would do him no good at all. Then, as night fell yet again, Wilfred, heir to the noble House of Dracula, slipped out of the castle. He took with him a jug to bring back his father's favourite tipple: human blood.

Wolves howled in the distance as Wilfred went down Bram Hill. He trembled, but on he went, down and down into the valley. He had no idea that his life was about to change – forever.

# Chapter 2
# Followed!

It was Wilfred's plan to go to the village. The villagers would be asleep at this hour, and with luck he would be able to tiptoe into cottage after cottage and take all the blood he needed from the necks of his victims without waking anyone. It was a suck and spit job.

Unfortunately, he had to pass through Stoker Wood to get to the village. No-one entered Stoker Wood at night unless they were either a vampire or very stupid indeed.

The trees in the wood creaked a lot, even though there was no wind. Unseen birds fluttered in the treetops above his head. Small creatures scurried and scuttled round his feet. Larger beasts moved about in the darkness, their eyes glowing like sly torches.

Wilfred gulped, but he gripped his jug all the more firmly, and on he went, deeper and deeper into the wood. He looked neither right nor left for fear of what he might see.

He'd been walking for about fifteen minutes when he noticed a small, regular sound some way behind him.

*Padda-pad. Padda-pad. Padda-pad.*

Wilfred paused. The small, regular sound paused too.

He began walking again.

*Padda-pad. Padda-pad. Padda-pad.*

He broke into a run. The small, regular sound also speeded up.

*Padda-padda, padda-padda, padda-padda, pad.*

And then? Wilfred tripped over a root and fell flat on his face.

And another sound joined the first.

*Pant-pant-panta-pant. Pant-pant-panta-pant.*

The hair on Wilfred's head sprang up, and so did he. To his feet, he sprang, and climbed the nearest tree until he reached a sturdy branch. His heart thudded madly as he looked down. An enormous wolf stood at the foot of the tree, staring up at him, licking its hairy lips.

"Ha!" jeered Wilfred. "Fooled you, Mr Wolf! You won't have *me* for supper tonight!"

He clapped his hands at his own cleverness. As he clapped, his elbow nudged something. Something big. Something with hot breath and wide, yellow eyes. Wilfred stopped clapping. He peered into the darkness.

On the branch, very near him, was a large, inky shape. What was it? For all he knew it was some wild creature that longed for a tasty snack of boy meat.

*"Waaaaaaaaaaaaaaaaaaah!"*

This was the sound Wilfred made as he toppled off the branch and fell into a pile of leaves. At the very feet of the wolf. The wolf growled hungrily – and pounced.

But as the wolf pounced, something odd happened. It should have torn Wilfred apart and swallowed his heart in a single gulp, but it did nothing of the kind. After pouncing on him, it simply lay there, on top of him, quite still, moving neither tooth nor muscle, ear or paw.

Wilfred, eyes firmly closed, lay beneath the heavy, unmoving wolf for some time expecting the worst. But when the worst didn't happen, he opened his eyes and prodded the beast gently.

"Mr Wolf, are you all right? Wolf? Nice wolfy."

Still the wolf did not move, so Wilfred eased himself out from under it. The wolf continued to lie there. This wasn't surprising, really, because there was an arrow in its back.

The wolf was as dead as a rusty doornail.

# Chapter 3
# The Night Hunter

Wilfred looked about him. Nothing moved. Nothing made a sound.

"H-h-h-hello?"

No reply. Not a word. Not a whisper. Not a burp.

Wilfred's spine tingled. The absolute silence and stillness worried him just as much as the *padda-pad, padda-pad* and the *pant-pant-panta-pant* of the wolf had done.

Once more, he kicked up his heels and ran for his life. As he crashed through the wood it seemed to him that something was running with him, keeping pace but never quite showing itself. Something wild and dangerous which could kill him as soon as look at him if it chose.

And then it was gone, whatever it was, and Wilfred was alone again.

Owls hooted – *oo-hoo, oo-hoo* – as if mocking him, and he came to a halt, breathing hard, wishing he was back home, snug in his coffin.

But then he remembered his plan to prove that he was a true vampire and make his father proud of him. He *must* get to the village.

Ah, but which way was the village? With all this mad dashing about, Wilfred had lost all sense of direction. He wandered this way and that for ages, but never came to the end of the wood.

Every now and then there was a movement ahead of him and he changed direction to avoid it. Then, a little later, he would sense a presence in the dark and would swerve again to avoid it.

All of a sudden Wilfred smelt something very unexpected in that haunted wood: roasting meat. He peered through the trees and saw the bright flicker of a campfire. He crept forward till he came to a clearing. In the clearing sat a boy.

The boy, who had his back to Wilfred, sat on a log roasting something over the fire. It was a squirrel, which looked as if it was crisping up nicely. Wilfred realised that he was hungry. Very hungry. He licked his lips. He could almost taste that squirrel.

But then he cursed his luck. He was a vampire. Vampires only eat cooked meat when there's nothing living to sink their teeth into.

He looked again at the boy. He wore a long black cloak with the hood thrown back. An easy matter, Wilfred decided, to sneak up, bite the boy's neck, and sip enough blood to take the edge off his appetite. Then he would squirt some blood into his jug before going on to the village for ...

The jug. Where was it? He looked about him. He couldn't remember dropping it or putting it down, but he no longer had it and that was a fact.

So now what? Perhaps the boy in the clearing had something he could use.
He couldn't ask, of course, because some of the blood he planned to take home was going to be the boy's. Perhaps if he drained off just enough to weaken the boy he could find a container, then squirt some more of his blood into it. Good plan!

Wilfred crept across the clearing until he stood behind the boy. He got ready to sink his fangs into his victim's neck.
But then the tempting smell of roasting squirrel pinched his nostrils and his knees sagged. Oh, why do I have to be a vampire? he thought. I would so much prefer leg of squirrel to neck of boy.

"So what are you waiting for?"

Wilfred jumped. The boy had spoken and now turned to look up at him.

"It's quite clean, you know," the boy said.

"Wh-what is?" Wilfred stammered.

"My neck. Washed it only last month. But you've missed your chance. You'll have to be quicker than that if you're going to bite me."

"How did you know I was behind you?" Wilfred asked. "How did you know what I was going to do?"

"Eyes in the back of my head," said the boy. "And I tell you, if your teeth had come within a nip of my neck you'd have needed a dentist the next instant. What's it all about? Think you're a vampire, do you?"

Wilfred stepped over the log and faced the boy.

"I don't *think* I'm a vampire. I *am* a vampire. My father is Count Dracula!"

Now this really did take the boy by surprise.

"Count Dracula is your father? But he's my hero! It's because of him that I became a night hunter."

"Night hunter?" Wilfred said.

"Someone who hunts by night. I'm good at it too. Always have been. From the moment I could walk, I wanted to stay out all night and sleep all day like the Count. My parents used to curse the very name Dracula. He set a bad example to young boys, they said."

"Don't your parents mind any more?" asked Wilfred, sitting down on the log.

"Not since the night of the storm, they don't," the boy said.

"What happened the night of the storm?"

"Lightning struck a tree beside the house. It crashed through the roof and flattened them in their sleep. I was out at the time – hunting."

"How sad," said Wilfred.

"Oh, it could be worse. I can go out whenever I want now, no questions asked." He glanced at Wilfred. "What are you called?"

"Wilfred," said Wilfred.

"My name's Smirk," the boy said, smirking. "Like a bit of squirrel? It's about done."

Wilfred shook his head. "I can't. Vampires don't eat cooked meat."

"That's a shame, I prepared it just for you."

"For me?"

"I was expecting you. In fact I guided you here."

"Nobody guided me," Wilfred said. "I just walked through the wood, walked whichever way I wanted."

"Mostly you ran," Smirk said. "And every now and then something made you swerve and go in another direction. That was me."

He tore a leg off the squirrel and offered it to Wilfred. Wilfred was so hungry by this time that he took the leg and, vampire or not, sank his teeth into it.

He rolled his eyes. It was the best thing he'd ever tasted.

He noticed Smirk watching him with amusement. "Aren't you having any?" Wilfred asked.

"No. I have no taste for dead flesh."

As if to prove this, Smirk snatched a mouse as it scurried by and popped it in his mouth. The little hind legs and tail stuck out between his lips, twitching. He crunched hard. The little hind legs and tail went limp. Smirk spat them out and chewed up the rest.

"You dropped this," he said then, and reached down beside him.

Wilfred stared. It was his jug, his own jug, the one he'd lost. "How did you come by this?"

"You dropped it when you climbed the tree to escape the wolf."

"You saw that?" Wilfred said.

"More than saw it. Where do you think the arrow came from?"

"If that was you, then I owe you my life."

"It was and you do," said Smirk. "Eat up now."

Wilfred did so, eagerly. The squirrel was so tasty, and the fire so cheering, that before long he grew quite drowsy.

"Feel free to take a nap," Smirk said.

"I can't. I have to go to the village. There's something I must fetch for my father."

"The night is young. Plenty of time for a nap *and* a trip to the village and back before dawn. Go on, have a little doze, you'll feel better for it."

The idea of a nap appealed to Wilfred. He curled up against a log, and very soon was sleeping like ... well, like a log.

# Chapter 4
# Smirk's Gift

Wilfred's eyelids felt warm. He opened them, to be almost blinded by sunshine. He flung his arm across his eyes in horror. "The sun! Oh no, the sun!"

Smirk stood nearby, the hood of his cloak pulled up over his head. "It doesn't seem to have done you much harm so far."

Wilfred lowered his arm and to his surprise the sunlight did not affect him. He'd never been out during the day before, so he had never felt the sun on his face, or watched it dance on the back of his hands.

"I don't understand," he said. "Father says daylight is harmful to vampires. And it's even worse when we're older. Then it turns us to dust. All my life he's told me that only normal people can survive during the day. People like you. Boring Normals, he calls you."

"Is this what you call *normal*?" Smirk said.

He tugged the hood back a fraction. His face was as pale as death, his eyes as red as cherry tomatoes. He looked ill. Very, *very* ill.

"I'm allergic to sunlight. It gets worse every year. When I was little, I stayed out at night and indoors between sunrise and sunset to be like the Count. Now I have to, like it or not."

"Why aren't you indoors now, then?"

"Because I wanted to see how the sun would affect a real vampire."

"But it might have done me serious harm," Wilfred said, in horror. "And you would have just stood there *watching*?"

"I was curious," Smirk said, and pulled his hood over his face again. "I've never met an actual vampire before. But the weird thing is, the sun doesn't seem to hurt you at all – unlike me, and I'm just a farmer's son."

Now Wilfred became excited. "Do you realise what this means? It means that all these centuries we Draculas have shut ourselves away in that gloomy, old castle when we could have been out and about. Just think, we could have been chatting to the neighbours, having picnics, boating on the river! I must go and tell Father at once!"

"I thought you had something to do in the village," Smirk said.

"Oh, this is much more important." Wilfred was keen to be off. "Goodbye, Smirk. Thanks for killing the wolf and cooking the squirrel. Perhaps we'll meet again some time."

"Can I come with you?"

"Come with me? No, no. The only visitors Father welcomes are those who want to donate blood. That doesn't include you, I imagine."

"No," said Smirk firmly. "Look, I just want a glimpse of him. I'll make sure he doesn't see me, I promise."

"Even if I agree," Wilfred said, "you don't look well enough to walk all that way."

"Who said anything about walking?"

Smirk raised his arms and his long cloak fluttered about him as if it had a will of its own. Then his feet left the ground.

Wilfred gasped. "Boring Normals aren't supposed to do that! Even I can't do it, and I'm a vampire. Father's tried to show me many times, but I never could get the hang of it."

"I've been able to do it since I was a toddler," Smirk said, "a sort of gift, I suppose, to make up for being allergic to sunlight. Take hold of my cloak."

Wilfred took hold of the cloak and his empty jug, and the next moment he and Smirk were rising through the trees.

Soon, the wood was a bright carpet of leaves beneath them. Wilfred's amazement turned to pleasure. He laughed and glanced at Smirk, but his new friend's face was hidden by the hood of his cloak. For an instant, the hood looked less like a hood than the head of a monstrous bat.

"Are you ready?" Smirk asked.

"Yes," said Wilfred.

"Then off we go!"

The cloak folded about Wilfred, flapped a couple of times like great, black wings, and then they were flying – yes, flying! – towards Castle Dracula.

# Chapter 5
# A True Vampire

Smirk said nothing more until they drew near the castle. "I've longed to visit this place," he said from deep within his hood. "Never quite found the nerve. Where do we find him, your noble father?"

"He'll be asleep by now," Wilfred said. "That's his coffin-room up there. The window next to the drainpipe."

"The shutters are closed."

"Closed against the light, that's all. They're not locked."

They came to rest on the wide window ledge. Wilfred pushed the shutters back just enough to see in.

"There," he whispered.

Smirk pressed an eye to the crack and saw his great hero snoring gently in his coffin. A shaft of light entered the room by the same crack, and touched the Count's hand.

"He'll be furious if he knows I've brought someone home with me," Wilfred said. "You'd better stay out here."

"Stay out here? You forget, I'm allergic to the sun."

"Oh, all right, go in then. But don't make a sound – and hide yourself."

Wilfred opened the shutters a little more and Smirk jumped in, silent as a cat, and tiptoed across the gloomy room.

While Smirk hid himself behind a heavy curtain, Wilfred also entered. But he was so eager to speak to his father that he left the shutters ajar. The sunlight followed him in as he went over to the coffin and shook the Count gently by the shoulder.

"Father, great news! It's not true that direct sunlight harms vampires. We can go out whenever we want! I've proved it!"

The Count frowned in his sleep. He stirred. His lips drew back to reveal two sharp teeth at the corners of his mouth.

"Who dares disturb my slumbers?" he growled.

"It's me, Wilfred. Come on, Father, wake up. You don't have to sleep during the day any more. Look, I'll show you."

The groggy Count sat up and scratched the back of his hand where the sun had touched it. What nonsense was the boy talking? The sun harmless? Had he lost his mind?

Wilfred ran to the window and flung the shutters wide. Sunshine flooded the room. The Count, elegant in his black silk pyjamas with 'CD' on the top pocket, scrambled out of his coffin in panic.

"Wilfred, what are you doing? Close the shutters!"

"It's all right, Father, don't worry, the light won't hurt you!"

The Count stepped forward, intending to rush at the shutters and slam them shut. But the sun fell full upon him and all energy drained out of him. As the golden glow bathed him from head to foot he drooped, and the wax in his hairy old ears melted and dribbled onto his shoulders.

"Oh, foolish boy!" he wailed, falling back.

Wilfred stared. "But why does the light hurt you and not me? I'm your son, your own flesh and blood. It doesn't make sense."

"But it does," said the Count. "I've suspected it for years, and this proves it. Close the shutters before it's too late. I have something to tell you, Wilfred."

But Wilfred was too excited to think about shutters. "Something to tell me? What, Father, what?"

"Remember the story I used to tell you at coffin-time about when you were a baby and Baron Gertler took the form of a bat and carried you off?"

"Yes, what of it?"

With the sunlight eating into him, the Count grew leaner and more wizened by the second. The skin shrivelled on his cheeks. His jaw stood out like a bent shovel. The bones of his wrists and elbows looked like knotted pipe-cleaners.

"I followed the Baron to a small farm," he said, with some difficulty. "He had a headstart on me, but I saw him carry you into the farmhouse before making his escape through a window. He paid for that night's mischief later. Oh, how he paid!"

The red gleam returned for a moment to his eyes as he remembered how he had defeated his old enemy. But then his eyes dulled once more. He gave a dry cough, and his chest caved in. "The shutters, Wilfred, the shutters."

"Oh, yes. Sorry, Father."

Wilfred slammed the shutters, but so eager was he to hear the rest of the story that he didn't close them properly. As he returned to his father's coffin-side, one of them swung slowly open again and light once more filled half the room – the half where the drooping Count sprawled against his coffin.

"Go on, Father, what happened then?"

"By the time I reached the farmhouse,"
the Count continued, breathing hard, "the
night was almost over. In minutes, the sun
would be up and I would be done for. I flew
into the house to scoop you up – and came
upon a cradle with *two* babies in it."

"Two?" said Wilfred, startled.

The Count's splendid pyjamas turned to rags in the golden light.

"In his haste to escape me," he went on, "the Baron had dropped you in the cradle he found in that room, next to the new child of the house. I had to decide – in great haste – which of the two was mine."

"But surely you knew which was your own *son*," Wilfred said.

"All babies look the same to me," the Count snapped. "I had to make a choice before the sun rose and destroyed me. I seized the one that seemed to have my nose and ... Wilfred, I hate to tell you this, but ..."

"You brought the wrong baby home."

"Seems I did," said the Count.

"So I'm not your son after all?"

"Seems not. Sorry, Wilf."

"Can it be so?" Smirk, the night hunter, stepped out from behind the curtain.

The amazed Count's brittle jaw almost shattered upon his chest.

"Who's this?" he demanded feebly.

"His name's Smirk," Wilfred told him. "We met in Stoker Wood. He saved my life and gave me a leg of roast squirrel. He's a big fan of yours."

"More than a fan, it seems," Smirk said, keeping to the shadows. "My mother often told me that I changed overnight when I was a baby, but she never thought for a moment that I might have been exchanged for her real son."

"Exchanged?" Wilfred said. "You were exchanged for *me*?"

Smirk's eyes were bright red and the teeth at the corners of his mouth looked very sharp. "It explains everything. My allergic reaction to sunlight. The fact that I can fly. My taste for live flesh. I'm not a Boring Normal after all. I never was. I'm the son of Count Dracula himself!"

# Chapter 6
# Dreams Come True

Risking the dreadful sunlight, Smirk darted from the shadows and hugged the withered old Count.

"Kiss me, Father!"

The hug was too much for the dying vampire. His ribcage cracked in several places. With his last breath he said, "Don't ... squeeze ... please ..."

Then Smirk was holding not a father but two armfuls of really old dust. He opened his arms and the dust fell to the floor. Shocked as he was, he remembered to go back into the shadows before the sun weakened him.

"If you are my father's real son," Wilfred said, wiping a tear from his cheek, "then ... who am I?"

"You," said Smirk, "are the only son of Dweeb van Helsing, the man I grew up calling Papa – or Miseryguts, depending on my mood."

"But he's dead too," Wilfred said sadly. "I'll never even meet him."

"Not unless you dig him up," Smirk replied. "But you have the farm."

"Farm?" said Wilfred.

"It came to me when Mama and Papa were killed. It's a bit of a mess because I never cared for farming myself but you're welcome to it. And I suppose I'd better move in here and become the new Count Dracula. Er ... you don't mind, do you?"

"Mind?" Wilfred cried happily. "This is wonderful! I don't have to prove anything any more. I'm not a vampire. Or even a wimpire. I'm a Boring Normal!"

"And I," said Smirk, "can stop feeling bad about not working in the fields and milking the rotten cows."

"You have cows?" said Wilfred in wonder.

"Five," said Smirk.

"Then I can have fresh milk every morning."

"You can have it till it pours out of your ears. And I, at last, have a good excuse to drink blood."

"I suppose we'll have to swap names too," Wilfred said.

"Let's not," said Smirk. "I don't see myself as a Wilfred somehow."

With these important matters settled between them, they fetched a broom and swept the dust of the late Count into an empty biscuit tin. Smirk put the tin on the mantelpiece in the dining room and made a solemn vow never to put biscuits in it.

Then Wilfred van Helsing, farmer's son, left Castle Dracula for the last time. He sang a cheery song and there was a spring in his step as he strolled down Bram Hill. Ahead of him lay the life he'd always dreamed of. A very ordinary life, in which

he could lie about in the sun all day, and sleep all through the night.

Oh yes, and not feel bad about preferring milk fresh from the cow to blood fresh from the neck.

# Who is Barrington Stoke?

Barrington Stoke was a famous and much-loved story-teller. He travelled from village to village carrying a lantern to light his way. He arrived as it grew dark and when the young boys and girls of the village saw the glow of his lantern, they hurried to the central meeting place. They were full of excitement and expectation, for his stories were always wonderful.

Then Barrington Stoke set down his lantern. In the flickering light the listeners were enthralled by his tales of adventure, horror and mystery. He knew exactly what they liked best and he loved telling a good story. And another. And then another. When the lantern burned low and dawn was nearly breaking, he slipped away. He was gone by morning, only to appear the next day in some other village to tell the next story.

# If you loved this story, why don't you read . . .

# Living with Vampires

## by Jeremy Strong

Are your parents normal? Kevin's parents are really odd. They can turn people into zombies. Blood is their favourite drink. Even worse, they are coming to the school disco! How can Kevin get his parents to behave normally so he can impress the beautiful Miranda?

You can order this book directly from:
Macmillan Distribution Ltd, Brunel Road, Houndmills,
Basingstoke, Hampshire RG21 6XS
Tel: 01256 302699

Barrington Stoke would like to thank all its readers for commenting on the manuscript before publication and in particular:

Tom Allen
Nile Bailey
David Barton
Ben Blake
Declan Blench
Emily Chomicz
Emily Clark
Rosemary Clark
Jimmi Davson
Sophie Dickson
Jack Finneran
Billy Frost
Jenny Garner
Jenny Gooch

Caroline Holden
Craig Johnson
Annie Kaufeler
David Lovegrove
Penny Martin
William Mathias
Kirsty McGeachey
Luke Myers
Danny Page
Julia Rowlandson
Heather Taylor
Ben Tuckwell
Scott Yates

## Become a Consultant!

Would you like to give us feedback on our titles before they are published? Contact us at the address or website below – we'd love to hear from you!

Barrington Stoke, 10 Belford Terrace, Edinburgh EH4 3DQ
Tel: 0131 315 4933 Fax: 0131 315 4934
E-mail: info@barringtonstoke.co.uk
Website: www.barringtonstoke.co.uk